Unexpected

Wounded Souls Novella

by
Amanda D. Lanclos

Amanda Lanclos

Published: Amanda Lanclos March 1, 2016

Editing: JoAnne Thompson

Cover Design: MGBookCovers

Formatting by: Brenda Wright, Formatting Done Wright

This book is intended for a mature audience of eighteen and older.

Dedication

This book is dedicated to every woman who has ever gone through infertility. It isn't an easy thing to battle and it doesn't make you any less of a woman. Remember, you are beautiful, in every way!

Amanda Lanclos

Table of Contents

Chapter 1

Heather

Five years ago, my life changed. My marriage was a testament to trying to live with a person who was as broken as I was, because I was unable to carry a child to term. Then, one angel came into my life bringing in her wake, a sea of emotions I never imagined I could have. After six miscarriages, Samantha was brought to our door from a mutual friend in Louisiana, scared and pregnant. She came to live with us as a favor to my Aunt Holly who was good friends with Sam's mother. And with her, came a new peace into my life, as well as my marriage with Declan. You see, her tragedy became my reality; my saving grace. A horrible event, granted my every wish. I felt for her, but I also knew that without her tragedy, you couldn't see the beauty in life. Sam gave me my reason for living. I became the mother I never dreamed I could be.

Sam's life was forever changed five years and nine months ago, but for me, mine changed five years ago – the day Isabella was born. Isabella, she was my beautiful miracle born from Samantha's horrible misfortune. You see Isabella was conceived out of a rape. Her mother came to live with us so that she wouldn't have people at home asking questions. While I was unable to carry a baby to term, Sam allowed one to grow inside of her because she couldn't imagine killing someone. She showed me what it was like to be strong. I allowed it, but I didn't think the feelings that came with having a pregnant woman in our house would take over the way they had - until that Christmas Eve when Sam came down and asked Declan and I, if we would like to adopt Isabella. It was a memory I would never forget.

I watched as Sam came into the living room, looking at the Christmas tree that was surrounded by presents. She was wearing a bright red sweater dress that hugged her baby bump that was just starting to show. She was almost five months pregnant and the most beautiful thing I'd seen. I envied her, but I also hated her at the same time – which of course was wrong of me considering she didn't ask for this to happen to her. She hadn't tried to bring this on herself; it just was what fate had in store for her. Just like fate had it in store for me to never know the depths of emotion for a child conceived from the love Declan and I shared, born after months of nurturing them in my own body. An unborn child, yes I knew the depths of that love. I loved each of those babies I had lost. Including the one I'd lost two weeks before Sam came to live with us.

"Declan, Heather, I have a present for you," Sam says softly as she reaches under the tree and grabs a medium-sized box with a red bow on the top.

"You didn't have to do that for us," Declan says softly as he takes the gift from her. Kate, our sister-in-law, had just left and was getting ready to pop with our nephew, Matthew, any minute. Okay, okay she had another month but the woman was massive. Her husband, Declan's brother Matt, was currently posted in Afghanistan.

"I know, but you've both brought me into your home. I was practically a stranger and had I known your situation, and how difficult this would be for you both, I wouldn't have come."

"Sam, we wanted you here," I interrupt her and she smiles.

"Mrs. Holly was a savior for me, just like the two of you are – but, I see it on your faces. You think you hide it well but it slips sometimes."

"I'm sorry for that, I do enjoy having you here. You've become a very dear friend."

"In this box, is something that, I hope, will make your generosity worth it. You've both given me so much by opening your home to me. This is what I want to give you in return." She gives us a smile as she runs her hand over her stomach.

Declan hands me the box, giving me an encouraging smile. "Why don't you go ahead and open it then, Heather."

*"Okay," I look at the box. Slowly, I pull the ribbon off, followed by the sparkling green paper. I open the box and inside is a heap of papers. I look down at them, a little confused until one word sticks out in my mind. **Adoption**. "What? Sam, we couldn't."*

"And give me one reason why you couldn't?"

"Why would you want us to?"

"This is something to show me that not every horrible situation has to end that way. I know you two will love her even though she wasn't conceived out of love. I love her enough to hope that her family will love her as much as she deserves. With the two of you, I know she will have that love."

I hand Declan the papers, both of us look at each other with tears pooling our eyes. I stand shakily, make my way to Samantha and wrap her into a huge hug. "You have just given me the greatest gift I could have ever received."

"Thank you so much," Declan says through his own sobs. Seeing my handsome and fearless husband the way he is right now

makes me weep for him as well. I wasn't the only one who was haunted by the possibility of never having a child to love and raise together.

"You are my angel," I whisper.

She will never truly know the gift she bestowed upon us that year and I could never show her how grateful we were to her. She married Jameson Carter a few years ago - who also had a huge part in our lives. He served in Afghanistan with my brother-in-law Matt and was there when we lost him. He went through many months of grieving and survivor's guilt that he lived, while Matt and three others, didn't. It was great seeing Sam and Jameson become one and they are now expecting their first child.

Sam also had a huge friendship with my sister-in-law Kate, because they had bonded while being pregnant at the same time. Mason had become such a huge part of our lives and he played a huge part in Sam's as well. He'd been the one to rescue her that horrible night. He was also an angel because he saved Kate. He'd stepped in and become a great role model for Matthew.

As for Declan and I, we'd all but stopped trying to conceive. While our sex life had never faltered, we both knew that I wouldn't be able to carry the child for as long as they needed.

Kate and Mason would be here any minute to pick up Isabella for the week, so that Declan and I could head to the cabin in Tennessee to celebrate our anniversary. September was always my favorite time to make it up to the cabin because of all the pretty colors that came with fall. It was something we'd done every anniversary since we'd gotten married ten years ago. This anniversary would be extra special; a decade together. I made sure to hide the perfect gift for Declan where he couldn't find it, and made a mental note to have it all planned out for when we arrived at the same cabin we'd rented for the past nine years. I swear that one day we will bring Isabella up here. Maybe in the winter, as I would love to see her beautiful blue eyes shine in the twinkling of the snow, as her blonde hair blows in the breeze. She looks more and more like Samantha as time goes on, but I can also see her features starting to resemble Alex –her sperm donor. Of the men who had savagely raped her that night over five years ago, he was the only one that felt any remorse for what he'd done while under the influence of alcohol and peer pressure. I am somewhat relieved that out of them all, it was he who fathered Isabella. Especially when you consider that we had to see him every now and then. His brother, Garrett, was dating Mason's sister Harlie.

I hear a noise in the living room so I hurry to hide Declan's gift in the bottom of my suitcase before walking out to check on the commotion. My breath halts in my chest as I take in the scene before me. Seeing Declan like this never ceases to amaze me. He's in his work uniform with his light blue button up shirt rolled up over his muscular arms. His jeans are fitted to perfection showing off his nice ass that I love to grab so much. When he turns to look at me, those silver grey eyes pierce into my very soul. If he weren't holding Isabella right now I would be humping him like a dog in heat. The man is sex on a stick and I was not unaffected by it, nor did I ever want to be.

He'd made me his wife ten years ago, which I still couldn't understand. I'm nothing special to look at; the curves of my hips were slightly bigger than other women and my ass didn't fit into a size two, much less a size twelve. I have average C-cup breasts. My mousy brown hair and eyes did nothing to distract from the freckles splattered over my nose and cheeks.

Declan bites his lip as if he knows exactly what's crossing my mind. I give him a knowing grin, because in less than ten hours he will get exactly what he wants. As will I.

I hear a horn sound and a car pulling up. I watch as Declan grasps a wiggling Isabella as she fights to get out of his arms to tackle Mason.

I can't help but smile over the life we have together. The only thing that could have made it even more perfect was to not be broken. To be able to offer Declan a child of his own flesh and blood, a child we created out of our love. That was something I tried hard not to dwell on too often.

I give myself a little pep talk as I watch Declan help Mason pack up Isabella's suitcase and toys into his car. "Heather, you can't change your past. You can't make yourself carry a child either. Let's count the blessings we do have; a wonderful husband, a beautiful daughter to raise together and our health."

Chapter 2

Declan

Driving up the slopes of the hills in Tennessee with the woman of my dreams is something that never gets old. Ten years ago she became my wife, ten beautiful years. Yes, there were issues with our marriage, some that almost caused us to lose the best thing we had in life – each other. Watching my wife go through all that we have suffered through over the last ten years, particularly in the beginning of our marriage was something I never wanted to witness. Seeing the light leave her eyes as the spotting and cramping started all over again hurt me emotionally as much as it hurt her physically. That was something that never got easier, even knowing I wasn't the one physically losing the child. Heather just wasn't able to carry a baby to term; the doctor really didn't have the answers for it. We just knew that after about sixteen weeks her body couldn't hang on.

I look over at her sleeping peacefully against the door, her long lashes resting on her cheeks as her eyes flutter from the dream she's having. Reaching over, I slide my fingers into hers. She sighs in content and my face breaks into a huge grin.

We may not have been dealt the best hand, but we overcame everything. Ten years was a long time to spend together. Especially with a life like the one I had. I had the most amazingly sexy wife, a beautiful daughter – even if she wasn't my flesh and blood, she meant more than anything to me. She was what brought my wife back to me. Heather became the mother she'd always dreamed of being and she shined through that role.

Today was a new day and I couldn't wait to give her the gift I'd gotten her for our ten-year anniversary. I steal glances at her sleeping beside me as we make our way to the Smokey Mountains. I can't help but smile.

I remember the day I met her, and I instantly knew that she would be my forever. I was seventeen years old when she came stumbling into the feed store I worked at, and I do mean stumbling, literally.

Her family had just moved to town a week ago and her car had broken down a mile up the road. They'd bought old Mr. Benny's farm, which needed more work than anyone here was willing to put into it, but it brought her here. She came into the store in boots and a pair of short cutoff jeans that would cause any man to have a stroke. I took one look at that girl and knew she'd be mine, but she wasn't looking at me in any way. I drove her back to her car even as she threw a fit, because she didn't need help from some "boy who kept ogling her." I finally won her over after getting the cracked radiator to stop steaming enough to get her car back to her family's house.

For a year I worked up my best game to win her heart and finally her senior year of high school she'd given it to me, along with her innocence. Ever since that day, I'd spent every minute of every day showing her exactly how good it would be with me.

As I pulled up to the cabin with the familiar wooden beams, green shutters and wraparound porch, ensconced with trees for seclusion, I felt the same anticipation in my body that I felt the first time we arrived here. Heather was in a white lace dress that hugged her perfect hips and curvaceous ass. That damn dress had driven me crazy the whole plane and car ride here. She'd taken her shoes off the second we'd climbed into the car and curled into herself. The wedding had taken a lot out of her, but it was a beautiful day and I had the most beautiful woman to bed as soon as I got her into the cabin. I remembered it just like it was yesterday and as I looked at the woman sleeping beside me now, I knew that I would never forget it, because those were memories that made the darker days of our lives that much brighter.

I turn off the engine and walk around the front of the truck to pick up my beautiful bride, much like I had ten years ago, scooping her into my arms and carrying her up the steps to the porch. Opening the door, I carry her past the newly refurbished kitchen. I barely spare a glance at the stainless steel appliances, granite countertops and dark-stained cabinets. Continuing down the hallway, I open the first door on the left, to the master suite, which contains the king-sized bed where we consummated our marriage ten years ago.

I smile as I remember the vividness of that night, two unsure lovers coming together to create something monumental. It wasn't really what I expected, especially after watching all the porn I had to prepare for the moment, but we were too completely imperfect people joining together in the perfect moment.

I lay Heather down on the white feather down comforter on the bed, before turning the bedside lamp on, basking her in light – making her look much like the angel I perceive her to be. She stirs, but doesn't wake as I make my way back out of the room to unload the car. After about thirty minutes I have the car and luggage all unloaded and ready for our stay.

I hear the floor creak and look up, my jaw hitting the ground as I take in the sight before me. Heather is standing there, her brown hair in waves of curls around her face and down her back. Her black lace negligee hugs her perfect body. I let out a low growl as I stalk her like the prey she is. She belongs to me and she knows it. She lets out a sultry laugh as I grab her by the hair, tilting her head back and joining our lips in a bruising kiss. When we pull apart her eyes are glossy and her lips are swollen from the attack mine just gave.

"Woman, when you look like that at me, it's hard to think straight."

"That's kind of the point, Dec. You're supposed to be so overcome with desire that you don't think about anything but me, naked, underneath your body," she says with a naughty grin as she slides her perfectly red manicured finger over my t-shirt clad chest. I grip her by the back of her thighs, lifting her as she wraps her legs around my hips. I take three long strides before I toss her onto the bed behind us. I watch in fascination as her hair flows over the pillows and her breasts bounce from the movement. I don't know what I ever did, but I thank God every day for bringing this beautiful soul into my life.

"Oh, well then it worked very well. You little temptress you," I smile as I lean down, running my nose up the length of her legs all the way to the apex of her thighs. I then spend the rest of the night showing my wife just how much love I have for her.

Chapter 3

Heather

Waking up to the smell of bacon is always one of my favorite things, but especially here in the cabin because Declan always cooks in nothing but those sexy briefs. I grab the box with the bright blue bow, from the bottom of the suitcase, noticing that he actually left it alone while unpacking. I walk uncertainly into the kitchen to give him the present I had made for him. I don't really know how he's going to like it, because it isn't something I'd normally give him. Heck, last year I got him that new shotgun he'd been begging for to go hunting with. I hadn't gotten him a gun in a very long time, not since Matt died. I was always afraid of what would happen with the guns we had, but I shouldn't have ever worried because Declan wasn't that type of man. I just knew that with our situation and then losing his brother, I wasn't sure if it would drive him to the edge. He'd taken to drinking for a little bit, but eventually stopped drinking when he saw how he behaved.

I never judged him for it though, because I didn't know what it was like to lose someone so close to you. I only knew the loss of losing your own child, to not be able to hear their heartbeat filling the room again. I shake the thought out of my head before the tears start to fall. I promised myself four years ago that I wouldn't let those feelings take over anymore, because I didn't want Isabella to know. When she was old enough to ask me why I was crying, I knew it was time to stop. I'd taken to alcohol at one point too; sometimes it was just easier to be numb.

I smile when I see his muscular back facing me, cooking the scrambled eggs I love so much. He always dices bell peppers really finely and throws them in with my eggs to make a sort of omelet.

"It smells good, but you look more delicious than that smells," I say as I wrap my arms around him, running my hands over the washboard of his abs before tracing the v and back up to his pecs. He grabs one of my hands and kisses it before turning to face me.

"Well, good morning Mrs. Jackson, you look exceptionally delicious this morning," he leans in and kisses my ear before licking it and whispering. "Much more delectable than last night and that's pretty damn hard to beat." I blush as I recall the events of last night that he's speaking of. He made sure he left no inch of me untouched and I'd loved every moment of it. He laughs as he sees the color creep into my face. "No need to be ashamed my love, it's all for me anyway."

"Very true," I smile and shove the gift into his hands. "This is all for you too," I bite into my bottom lip as I stand there nervously hoping he likes his gift.

"Well, I will just have to see what this is all about. But... you need to open yours too." He gives me a grin as he places the box on the counter. Declan grabs two plates and puts our food on them. Once he's sitting at the bar, I shakily grab the box again, placing it into his hands. "Why are you so nervous?"

"It's something you probably wouldn't expect of me," I say nonchalantly as he opens the box, revealing the eight by ten picture album of the boudoir photo shoot I had done. He could thank his sister-in-law for this, because had she not done one for Mason at the same time I wouldn't have done it either. I watch his face as he opens it and his eyes widen at the first picture. I had to admit it was my favorite; my eyes glowed as I looked over my shoulder with my ass in a black and pink lace hipster style panties and nothing else. My hair was curled and the artist there had done my makeup flawlessly. I had never felt more beautiful than I did during this photo shoot and by the look in his eyes and the bulge in his pants; it has done exactly what it was supposed to do.

"Holy shit, Heather. You had one of these done for me?" He never takes his eyes off of the album as he continues to flip through the pictures of me in various poses and lingerie. "Please tell me you kept this wardrobe." He looks at me and the desire shining through those amazingly sexy eyes has my core weeping. I shake my head yes as he sets the book down and prowls toward me. Yes, he prowls. I don't even have time to think as he lifts me from the floor and storms back to the bedroom, showing me again for the third time since we had arrived yesterday, what I mean to him. The only difference is this time he lets out his inner caveman and he shows me exactly who I belong to – and I love every damn minute of it.

We emerge out of the bedroom an hour later to cold eggs and greasy bacon. I muster the courage to swallow the unappetizing food. Declan laughs as he pulls the plate out of my grasp, taking it to the trash and dumping its content.

"Hey! I was eating that!" I mumble as he turns and gives me a blatant stare.

"I'm going to make my woman fresh food, you aren't eating that cold shit," he kisses my nose as he hands me a box. I look at him as he smiles a charismatic smile, the same one that knocked me to my knees so many years ago. I finger the wrapping paper on the box, slowly removing the bow. "Come on woman, open the gift. You're making me nervous as hell."

I ignore him as I slowly undo the ribbon, lift the lid on the box and stare at the charm bracelet. My eyes immediately fill with tears as I take in each little set of wings on the beads. In the center of each wing contains a jewel with the month of the due date of each child we were never able to bring into the world. "Do you like it?" He asks uncertain of the gift he chose and I just break down.

"It's. The. Best. Present. Ever." I say through broken sobs. He wraps me in his arms and wipes at my tears as they continue to fall down my face. I look up at him and I am sure that in this very moment, he can see into the depths of my soul. He may not know it yet, but this was the step I needed to fully heal. Isabella had started the healing process, but having Declan show me that I am not the only one who needs to remember our beautiful creations is awe-inspiring.

"Good, now let me cook you some hot breakfast, because with what I have planned for you later on, you're going to need some sustenance." He gives me a cocky grin as he turns toward the stove to make some fresh eggs and bacon.

Our week at the cabin seemed to fly by, but it was a very much-needed break for Declan and I. It had become harder and harder to have alone time with Isabella lurking in all the secret places we'd once used. For example, the laundry room, that child never set foot in the laundry room for years because of the sounds of the dryer. Declan had used that to his advantage many times and to be honest I kind of missed that spot. The banging of the old washing machine and dryer would keep our sounds at bay while we rekindled the love we never let waiver.

For a year or so, our love had started to take a turn for the worse, because of my infertility. Losing child after child for two years would begin to take a toll on anyone, but somehow our love for each other always seemed to prevail. I'd tried fertility drugs as well as other procedures but it never worked for us and after spending thousands of dollars we both accepted that children just weren't meant for our future. When we were twenty-three, Isabella came into our lives and turned it upside down. The pattering of feet that I so missed when we came to the cabin for the week, to the toothless grin she was sporting in the pictures her Aunt Kate would send, made me long for our home. As I sit at the counter in the kitchen my mind wanders to the first of many times we lost our child.

Declan and I wait in the waiting room of the doctor's office, excited to see the baby again. We'd already picked out its name. If it was a girl it would be McKenzie Rae and if it was a boy his name would be Holden James. When the nurse called my name, we both stood holding hands as we walked toward the ultrasound room to see our sweet baby.

"Are you ready for this?" I asked, since I'd come alone the first time just to confirm that I was indeed pregnant. I hadn't wanted to get his hopes up and have it be a false positive on the test.

"More than ready," his huge grin even had the nurse flabbergasted.

"Well then, let's see our baby."

"Mrs. Jackson, if you'll climb up here on this bed and lay on your back with your shirt up and Mr. Jackson, if you'll just have a seat in this chair beside it, we'll get started." Olivia smiles and those bright

green eyes seem to sparkle even more when they meet Declan's face. I normally wouldn't like the look she's giving him, but when he's so overjoyed it's hard not to.

"Yes ma'am," he takes his hat off his head and sits in the chair beside where I am lying, grabbing my hand and kissing my fingers. Take that, Olivia.

"Let's get started," she smiles as she squirts the warm gel on my stomach, she looks at the screen and tinkers with the machine for a moment before looking up at me. "I need to go grab something out of the other room, can you give me one moment? I'm so sorry," she gives me a small smile and in that instant I know that something isn't right. I just nod my head, not sure what it is.

A few minutes later, Doctor Nicholson comes in and the dreaded feeling I felt when Olivia was in here increases times two hundred.

"You must be Declan, nice to meet you. I'm Doctor Nicholson. I'm just going to come and do a little check on the ultrasound." She shakes Declan's hand before walking over to me.

"What's wrong?"

"Always so inquisitive." She gives me a smile, that doesn't reach her eyes. "Olivia couldn't get a heartbeat on the baby, so I'm going to see if I can't locate it. Sometimes things like this happen and it's just hard to tell with the baby being so small. Nothing to worry about."

"What if you can't find it?" Declan questions and my eyes fill with tears, I already know the answer to that because I can feel in my whole being that I've lost my baby.

"What's on your mind, beautiful?" I turn to look at the gorgeous man in front of me, sporting a five o'clock shadow and those stunning eyes of his. The smile across his face is something that still to this day sends the butterflies flurrying in my belly. I never expect that to dwindle either. God sent this man for me, I believed that one hundred percent.

"Just missing home," I give him a small shrug as he wraps me into his strong arms. I instantly feel safe as I inhale the musky essence of him mixed with the Hugo Boss cologne he's wearing. He tilts my chin up and gives me the softest kiss on the lips, one that shows me just how much I mean to him. Declan can make me feel like the most delicate piece of glass and then in an instant turn a switch that shakes my whole body to its core. He knows just when I need to be taken hard or loved sweetly and that's just another reason we mesh so well together.

"Well, maybe we should have just one more rendezvous," he wriggles his eyebrows as the square set of his jaw comes into my view, only to disappear as he kneels in front of me. He takes my flip flops off my feet one at a time, kissing up the inseam of my arch, causing my eyes to roll into the back of my head and a very un-lady like moan to roar through my chest. "That's it kitty, you just make those noises while I take care of you," he mumbles between kisses. He reaches for my hand and kisses the charm bracelet I will never take off and I swear if he wasn't holding my foot, I'd have melted into a puddle. It doesn't take him long to make me forget about missing home, because with him near me, beside me or inside of me, there is nothing that I ever need more than that. He is my home.

Chapter 4

Declan

Getting back into the groove of things took a while, but finally after a month after our return, our routine was back into place. I'd taken on longer hours at work so that I could save up so we could afford a trip to Disney World for Isabella's Christmas gift and though Heather offered to get a job while Isabella was in school – I wouldn't have it.

I'd recently noticed things that Heather was trying to hide from me. Like the fact that her eyes had dark circles underneath them and that at night she wasn't sleeping as well as she used to. She was tossing and turning more and becoming more restless, often leaving the bed so her restlessness wouldn't bother me. She'd also been losing some weight, which I was worried about more so now, than ever. Heather always had self-esteem issues, even with me not being able to keep my hands off of her. Isabella was excelling in school and Heather was doing everything she could with Isabella, while trying to hide the fact that something was terribly wrong with her. If it weren't for the dark circles and the restlessness she might have been able to keep it from me and for now I was allowing her to think I knew nothing.

I'd been working so much that I barely got to see her to have a conversation anyway. I would wake up at six to leave for work by seven, before she was even up with Isabella, and then I would return around seven just in time to eat and put Isabella down to bed and pass out in front of the television with a beer. Tonight was no different, other than Heather climbing into my lap and curling into me. I sighed in content as I wrapped my hands around her slender waist and rested my hands on her stomach. Moments like these made the struggle of day-to-day life worth living. I rubbed her stomach slowly as her breathing evened out, her chest rising and falling with each breath.

"Tired baby?" I smile as she lets out a hmpfh, before her head drops to the crook of my neck, nuzzling in to me. I inhale the sweet scent of her; strawberries and mango. The woman had a thing for fruity body wash. I maneuver her to where I can carry her, slipping my arms under her knees and standing. I try to be as quiet as I can so that I don't cause her to wake up, or wake Isabella up, in the process. Softly laying her on the bed, I watch as her eyes flutter and a soft smile overtakes her beautiful face. I don't know what the hell made me be the luckiest bastard in the world, but with this woman beside me, that is exactly what I am.

I wake up from a bad dream with a jolt as I try to catch my breath. I look over to see that Heather isn't in the bed anymore and I instantly freeze. I hear something in the bathroom and I begin to relax, but dreaming of seeing her lying in that casket was harder than I could have imagined. That nightmare, it shook me to my core, because a life without her was one not worth living. I tried to shake it as she opened the door to the bathroom, her eyes glossy as she walks over to the bed.

Amanda Lanclos

"I didn't mean to wake you," she says weakly as she climbs back into bed. *Oh baby, I wish it had been you that woke me.* "I was trying to be quiet. I think I'm sick."

"It's okay, you didn't wake me, but what's the matter?" I reach for her, concern etched on my face as I feel the clamminess that has taken over her body.

"I think I have a stomach virus, I'm so nauseous," she curls into a ball and wraps herself into the blanket as she tries to smile at me – almost like she is trying to reassure me.

"Want me to get you some Sprite and crackers?"

"No, I'm okay. I just need to starve it out," she closes her eyes and I sigh. It's going to be a longer night than I'd have wanted, because there is no way I am going back to sleep – especially not after that dream.

I lay in bed watching over her as she tosses and turns, I wish I could express my feelings without pissing her off, but I know that she's not going to listen. She's bull-headed and stubborn as all get out. But that resolve was one of the main things that made me fall in love with her and something I would never want to change about her. When we got into fights, it made the making up that much better. With Isabella and work though, the lovemaking had come to a catastrophic stop this last month since vacation. I'd become more acquainted with my hand than any married man should ever want to be. Finally, her eyes flutter close and she eventually falls into a peaceful sleep. For me though, I watch her sleep, almost as if she would really be gone if I closed my eyes. I will need a huge ass pot of coffee later if I want to make it through the day.

Kate walks into my office wearing a black tank top and one of those horribly unattractive maxi skirts. I don't know what the hell the deal is with those things. I look up at her as I sip my fourth cup of coffee today.

"I'm worried about Heather," she says. *Well don't even say hello. Let's get down to business.*

"Well, good morning to you dear sister-in-law." I cross my ankle over my right knee as I take another sip, preparing myself for the talk, or chewing out that I am fixing to get.

"Don't Declan! I know you can see something isn't right too! What are we going to do?" She slams her hands down on my desk and I flinch.

"Nothing I can do." I make sure she's looking right at me before I continue. "She has to realize something is wrong first, and she refuses. I think she's worried it's something bad and she's running scared. She will go see a doctor when she thinks the timing is right."

"It could be too late by then Dec!"

"Like I don't know that!" I yell, effectively shutting up the only other woman I have ever cared for. She was the sister I had never had, Kate was married to my brother Matt, but when he died it ripped a hole in all of us. He'd taken a piece of all of our souls with him the day he left this world. "I can't make her do it though, I don't want her to resent me for it."

"Dec, I don't think she would. She's not eating as much, she's barely sleeping. I can see it in her eyes. She's afraid, and she has every right to be. Didn't one of her dad's aunts have some form of cancer?" I shake my head yes as she keeps going. "I'm just trying to prevent you from ending up just like I did. Without the better part of your half." She gives me a sad smile before turning to leave.

"Thanks for that," I mutter as I try to think about the pain of losing my wife. The one person in the world who makes it great - she makes me want to be a better man and a better father. A world without her in it is a world filled with no color, it would be black and white. Running a hand over my face and exhaling loudly I sit there wondering what the hell I would do if it were cancer. I don't know if I could be strong for her, because in reality I'd be losing so much more than her – I'd lose myself, my reason for living.

Chapter 5

Heather

"Isabella, can you come in here and help me?"

"What do you need, Momma?" Her bright eyes shine as she comes into the kitchen. I try to not sway as I look into her face, her little smile lighting up my day.

"Would you bring momma a cup of water?"

"Sure Momma, you feeling bad?" She puts her little hand on my forehead and looks into my eyes. "Momma, you're all sweaty. Should I call Daddy or Aunt Kate?"

"My little Momma, you will make a good one, one day." I pat the couch beside me and she sits down, grabbing my hand. "How about instead, we just lay on the couch, snuggle and watch Frozen?"

"Deal, but let me get water for you. Can I have a bag of chips?" Her heart shaped face lights up and I can't tell her no. I nod my head as she runs into the kitchen.

"Here you go momma," she puts the water in my hand and begins to open the chips. The smell of the Cheetos has me running to the nearest bathroom, I really thought this stomach bug would go away, but it doesn't seem to want to let up. When I come back into the room, she looks at me with a frightened expression and I give her what I think is a reassuring smile, but the look on her face tells me that it was anything but.

"I'm okay baby, I'm just not feeling so well."

"It's okay momma, I'll put these up and we can watch Frozen. I'll go make a Hot Pocket after you go to sleep," she throws the blanket over me as I lay down and put my feet near her. We both cuddle into the couch as the sounds of Frozen lull me to sleep.

I wake up later surrounded by the scent of Declan, that musky essence that is all him, mixed with his Hugo Boss cologne. I'm burning up and I feel like I can't move. I stir a bit before realizing I'm not on the couch anymore, but in the bed and Declan's arm is the reason I'm restricted. I lie back on the pillow and try to get comfortable when I feel his lips against my ear.

"I'll move if you want." His gravelly voice fills my ear and I shiver instantly.

"No, don't. I like it here, but I'm so hot can I take off the blankets?"

"I think we can arrange that," he moves his arm before pulling the covers back and then wrapping me up in his strong arms. I can't help but smile because he is mine. He has and always will be mine.

"Thank you," reaching for his hand I kiss the knuckles of each finger.

"You're welcome, now if you don't stop doing that I won't be held accountable for my actions."

"Oh!" I feel his erection against my bottom and I try not to wiggle around because I am not really feeling one hundred percent.

"Besides, we need to have a long talk in the morning, so it's best if we get some sleep tonight." He pulls me tighter into him as my whole body goes rigid. "It's nothing like that, just go to sleep Heather."

Just go to sleep? How the hell am I supposed to go to sleep now? I look at the clock on the nightstand beside me. I watch as the red numbers slowly change minute by minute. I don't remember what happened after the clock hit two forty-five. I suppose I fell asleep because the next thing I remember was waking up to an empty bed and cold sheets from where Declan hadn't been for a while. I look back at the red numbers on the clock and see that it's nine thirty. I wonder why the house is so quiet on a Saturday morning and how in the world I managed to sleep past eight.

Getting out of the bed, I grab the fluffy coffee cup robe that Kate had gotten me a few years ago, slip my feet into my flip flop slippers and make my way down the hall to the kitchen. Declan is pacing back and forth behind the bar, running his fingers in his hair when I clear my throat. He looks up at me, as if he's a deer caught in headlights and my stomach drops. *"It's nothing like that Heather, just go to sleep."*

"Are you cheating on me?" I blurt and he looks at me as if I've lost my mind.

"Heather? Are you kidding me right now?" He raises his voice and slams his hands down on the counter. I jump because he's never really gotten angry with me.

"Well, you've been working later and later and you said we had to talk, I just," I shut up as he stalks toward me, grabbing my ponytail and attacking my lips with a bruising kiss. If I wasn't sure who owned my soul before, I was now. He pulls away and walks back to the counter.

"Heather, no. What we need to talk about is... you." His silver eyes bore into mine and I swear I feel as if the black abyss could swallow me whole. I want to disappear; I'd rather discuss him cheating than the sickness within me.

"I don't want..." I jump as he slams his hands again.

"Dammit Heather! I don't care if you want to talk about it or not!" He seethes, his veins popping out on the sides of his neck as he growls at me. "You aren't sleeping, you're losing weight. You look bad, baby."

"I'm fine," I stand ramrod straight as I look into his eyes. "I have a stomach bug." Crossing my chest and baring my teeth I hiss. "God forbid I not be this perfect trophy wife for you."

"Heather! I'm not talking about my attraction to you!" He grips the counter as he stares at me. "What's the matter?"

"Nothing!"

"Why won't you be honest with yourself? Something isn't right. How long have you been hiding this from me?" He lets go of the counter and walks over to me, wrapping me into his arms and rubbing his hand down my back. "What are you so afraid of?"

"I don't want to die," I finally break down and sob into his chest, my fingers gripping his shirt while he rubs my back.

"Baby, you're not going to die."

"I'm afraid I have cancer, Declan." Looking into his shocked face I know he finally grasps the severity of the situation.

"Why would you think that?" He grips the counter as his ashen face slowly lifts to meet my own.

"Why wouldn't I Dec? I've been sick for a few weeks now; I'm starting to swell up like a freakin' pumpkin. All I want to do is sleep. When Aunt Marlene found out she had cancer her symptoms were just like mine."

"Baby, you need to go..." he starts but I freak out.

"I'm not going to the doctor! I'm not having them tell me what I already know!" I scream out at him, my whole demeanor changing. I've never acted this way before, but I don't want to die. I break down and fall to the floor in tears as my whole body shakes. "I don't want to die," I whisper as he wraps me in his strong arms.

"Heather, baby you're not going to die. But, we need you to get to a doctor. Baby, even if it is cancer, early detection and treatment is important to beat it. It's not like it was years ago when Marlene was diagnosed." He rubs my cheeks as the tears fall. I don't know what he wants to hear because I keep telling him I'm not going, but he's not listening.

"I'm not going. I don't want to hear what I already know deep down."

"But we don't know."

"I'm not going. End of discussion," I know I'm being a stubborn woman, but that's always been my greatest asset when it comes to Declan. He avoids confrontation and I know it, so when he tries to reason with me, I become the bull-headed woman he fell in love with thirteen years ago.

"I'll let you win for now, but if you keep getting sick, Heather, I swear to God I will throw you over my shoulder caveman style and carry you to the doctor," he wipes the hair from my face as he watches me. "I can't lose you too."

"If I'm not better in a couple of weeks I'll make an appointment with a doctor," I bite on my fingernail as he looks at me.

"Deal. I'll give you two weeks."

"Fine, now will you make love to me?"

"Make-up sex at its finest. I like your thinking Mrs. Jackson," he grins as he picks himself up off the floor before lifting me up in his arms and carrying me to our bed.

He places light kisses all over my legs before sliding them over my swollen stomach and up to my breasts. He smiles as he continues to pull the shirt over my body and tossing it onto the floor. I whimper as he slides his own t-shirt off of his body and the v that I love so much peaks out of the top of his shorts. I slide a finger over one of the indentions, which earns a rumble from his chest. His lips attack mine as the rest of our clothing disappears from our body in a quick haste. He slides into me in one swift movement causing me to arch my back and take him even deeper inside me.

"This is where I belong, inside of you, like this. You were made for me, Heather Raye," his eyes blaze into mine and all I want to do is cry.

"Yes I was Declan Tate," I fight back the tears, because they aren't just happy ones and I don't want to ruin this moment for us. I want to be in the present as he slides in and out of me, showing me just how much I mean to him with every pump of his hips into my own. I don't want to remember that awful moment in our kitchen that happened less than five minutes ago. I don't want to think about the fact that what could be wrong with me could also be killing me. I want to stare into the face of this beautiful man before me and fall in love with him all over again. My fingernails graze the skin of his deliciously muscular shoulders as I arch into him. I can feel my own climax starting to build as I feel him starting to throb inside of me.

"I can't hold it anymore baby," he grunts out. I throw my head back as if his words detonate the release that's been building inside of me. I can't help but shake as his body starts to release. I swear I fall in love with that man a little bit more every day.

Chapter 6

Declan

Three weeks have flown by since the last talk I had with Heather about her health and things seem to be looking up. I've tried to work earlier in the morning instead of later at night so that I can be there to help her more with Isabella. If I hadn't known any better I would really think all of her symptoms were from pregnancy. I'd seen Heather pregnant enough times to know, but the doctor told her after the last miscarriage that it would be damn near impossible to even conceive again. Her womb just wasn't made to handle it.

She didn't know it, but I wasn't just working late to save up for our trip to Disney World, but I was also saving money to upgrade her wedding band. When we'd gotten married we didn't have a lot of money – not that we do now either, but she'd gotten a small third of a karat ring. It wasn't much but at the time it was all I could give her and to her, it was the prettiest damn ring on the planet. Her engagement ring was a simple white gold band and an emerald cut diamond in the center. Her band was a small half-karat band of diamonds and this year I was upgrading it.

I'd picked out this beautiful princess cut ring that has a karat of diamonds on the band and the big diamond was two karats. The wedding band had a karat that matched the engagement ring and it was breathtaking. The minute I saw it at the local jewelers I knew it was meant to be on Heather's finger. I'd been making monthly payments on it for three months now. I still had three thousand to pay off and planned to get it paid off before Thanksgiving, which was in three weeks. I was getting a bonus because of all the extra work I'd been pulling around at the plant and I hadn't told Heather because I wanted to surprise her with the ring.

Driving up to the house I laugh when I see Heather and Isabella outside raking leaves. I laugh because it seems like Isabella is strewing them more than she's raking. Her face lights up as she jumps into the sea of leaves heaped into a gigantic pile. I can see her long blonde curls peeking out of the leaves as she throws more in the air. I laugh as Heather throws her hands in the air with an 'oh what the heck' look and jumps into the sea of leaves with her. Climbing out of the truck, I run for the pile of leaves and the two people that hold my heart. I jump into the leaves with a huge "ARHHHHH!"

"Daddy!" Isabella jumps and wobbles through the leaves until she is in my arms and I'm throwing her into the leaves again.

"You're home early," Heather smiles as she kisses my lips before we are both tackled by the overly excited eight-year-old.

"Daddy! Can we go to a movie?"

"How about I do ya' one better?"

"Oh?"

"Yep, go call Uncle Mason and Aunt Kate and see if they want to come with us."

"Ok!" She squeals as she runs toward the house, slipping on the leaves as she goes.

"What's up your sleeve Mr. Jackson?" Heather raises an eyebrow and puts her hands on her hips.

"Remember that old projector Pop has?"

"Mmmmhmm."

"Think it's about time it's gotten some use. Don't you?"

"Okay, I guess I better get to making some snacks. Where you gonna put it?"

"Back by the oak tree. I think we could just bring the trucks and set up some pillows and blankets. Be like old times," I smirk and give her a pat on the bum as I walk past her to head into the shed.

Three hours later everyone is here. Mason and Kate brought his sister, Harlie, and her boyfriend, Garrett, with them since they were in town visiting. I'd been an ass the day I met Garrett because of who his brother was. I was always afraid that Alex would come back and try to take Isabella; after all it was his paternal right. So when I'd found out that Garrett was my daughter's biological uncle it scared the shit out of me. I wasn't prepared for the relationship that came with him knowing Mason, would alter our lives so much. I respected the hell out of the man and after voicing my concerns we'd all hashed it out and decided we would be able to make this work.

"Hey Dec!" I look up to see Kate walking up with Matthew running behind her screaming out.

"Uncle Declan!" He runs and jumps on top of me, almost sending us both falling to the ground. It always made me laugh and with those gangly limbs he reminded me more of his Dad daily.

"Hey little man, you're growing up on me."

"Yep, I'm gonna be just like my Dad when I'm older."

"I know you will, little buddy," he swats at my hand as I mess up his hair. "You just remember, you'll always be my little buddy."

"Yeah! Yeah! Isabella!" He takes off toward Isabella and sits down beside her in my truck bed. I look around as I see Heather and Harlie coming down with the trays of hot dog buns, wieners and the stuff for s'mores.

"How is she?" Kate whispers as I watch her.

.

"She's doing better. I think she just was going through something."

"Or she's good at hiding things."

"She's never been a good liar, Kate."

"Look, I just think there is still something going on. Something she isn't really telling anyone about. It isn't just you Dec."

"Hey you two!" Harlie smiles as she puts her tray down on the table. "This is a really fancy setup you have here, Declan."

"Thanks, it's been forever since we've used it."

"Since Matt was here," Kate says softly and I grab her arm. "No, it's okay. We need to be able to do things like this still." She smiles and kisses my cheek before going to help Heather.

"Well, I didn't mean to make things awkward. I just wanted to say thank you for inviting us," she rocks back and forth on her feet as she looks up. "I know it's still a tough situation."

"It's okay. We're glad to have you. I mean you are both family," I wince a little and she pats my arm.

"She never has to know. He's okay with that."

"Thank you," I smile as I look at the screen. "Well what are we waiting for? Let's cook some hotdogs and watch some 'Pitch Perfect 2'!"

Amanda Lanclos

We all walk to the bonfire of burning wood and the pile of leaves that Heather, Isabella and I finished raking and brought into the back by the big oak tree and the barn. We'd hung the projector and gotten everything ready just in enough time to take our baths before everyone got here. Shower sex when you're in a rush is amazing too. I love having the water dripping around us both and my hands sliding over her beautiful body as we make love around the steam. It also drowns out our noises so Isabella doesn't know what's going on.

"Dude, stop thinking about stuff like that. You're drooling like she's the best steak you've ever eaten and it's kind of making me not want to eat this hot dog anymore." Mason slaps my back as I laugh.

"Shut the hell up," I mutter as I turn my attention back to the here and now.

"Kate seem upset to you tonight?"

"The last time we did one of these was a couple of nights before Matt left," I look away from him as he gets quiet, just thinking.

"Right, now I get it."

"Look man, I didn't think about it. I was just trying to get..."

"It's okay. We all have to move on, I'm not mad. She needs those memories, and I need her." He interrupts me. "But, thank you for giving me the chance to give her more memories with me in them."

"Anytime."

Everyone eats then piles into the truck beds for two hours of laughter brought to us courtesy of snarky women and corny men who sing. I'll admit the movie wasn't as bad as I thought it would be and we'd all enjoyed a beautiful November evening under the stars. As I hold Heather in my arms I recall Kate's conversation in my office and I can't help but wonder if she knows something I don't.

Chapter 7

Heather

Thanksgiving seemed to sneak up on me, between Isabella's dance classes and trying to hide the fact that I still wasn't feeling well from Declan. I'd tried to ease myself out of the bed at night when I'd felt a need to catch my breath, or when I'd started to sweat. I'd started putting on facial masks while everyone was out of the house to keep him from seeing the bags under my eyes and I'd started wearing baggier clothing so that he couldn't tell I was losing more weight.

I'd just taken the turkey out of the oven when I hear the commotion of people coming into the house. We'd invited everyone here today because we had the open floor plan and enough space to hold everyone in our house. When Declan had built the house, he'd built it with a bigger family in mind. Now, we had to walk into the huge five-bedroom house with only one daughter to fill it with.

"Hey Heather!" Sam smiles as she wraps her arms around me in a hug.

"Hey! How are you doing? Where's my Gage?" I look around for the one-year-old and can't find him anywhere.

"He's with his Daddy, you know how those two are," she looks around. "What can I help you with?"

"Absolutely nothing. I have a few more things to get out of the oven and then it will all be ready. Are Blake and Anna coming?"

"Yeah and they have a surprise."

"Oh yeah?"

"Mmmhmm, OH!" She yelps as Jameson smacks her ass.

"Quit telling other people's business." He wraps me up in a hug and laughs as Sam growls. "Happy Thanksgiving, Heather."

"Thank you, you too. You're doing so much better on your prosthetics Jameson."

"When you have the best physical therapist for a wife, it's hard not to." He winks at Sam before I hear someone calling for him.

"Must be Mason. I gave Gage to him. Thought he'd need some practice." He winks and walks out of the room.

"I'm glad you found your happiness, Sam. You deserve it after you brought me mine."

"You're going to make me cry and we both know that isn't me. So let's stop," she smiles. "I should go check on Gage."

Once again I find myself alone in the kitchen. Everyone else is in the living room conversing and having a good time. I can't help but think that this is what it would be like without me here at all. I put my hands on the counter and try to hold back the tears that want to fall. I can't keep going on like this, I should listen to what Declan says, but it's the fear of the unknown that is holding me back. I don't even realize someone is standing beside me until I feel a hand wrap around my own and I meet those emerald eyes that have always been there for me.

"Gonna tell me the truth today?"

"Kate, I don't know what you want me to say."

"That you're scared. That you're afraid that you'll hear the words that you don't want to. That you're worried that you'll leave Declan alone and that you'll miss out on their lives?" She pulls me toward her and wraps me into a hug. "Or maybe that you've been trying to hide the fact that something isn't right and you aren't fooling me?"

"Kate, I'm fine. I've just been having some stomach trouble. I'm going to be fine."

"You need help, Heather. You're not sleeping, you're losing weight but your stomach is poking out more and more. Maybe it isn't what you think, what if you're pregnant?"

"I just had a cycle."

"Liar," she smiles.

I think back to the last cycle I had, but they have always been so extremely off balance that I can't really remember, but there is no way I'm pregnant. She gives me a smile and then looks at me.

"Heather, what were you thinking about in here?" Her hands go on her hips and I know she means business.

"Nothing," I mutter, thankful when the timer goes off on the oven, signaling that my dinner is now ready. "Food's ready!" I holler as I give Kate a small smile, thankful to end the conversation as everyone piles into the room.

"Oh man, this looks yummy!" Anna's voice comes over the loud chattering and I turn to look at her.

"Anna! Holy moly! You're huge!" I slap a hand over my mouth as she laughs, her whole belly shaking.

"Well, we wanted to surprise everyone. We haven't seen Kate and Mason or the two of you. Just Jameson and Sam knew since they've been visiting more." She smiles.

"I need to go back to get my ears lowered more often," Mason drawls and I laugh.

"You look absolutely stunning. I'm sorry for my lack of a filter."

"It's okay, I'm not ashamed. Now, me and these babies want some food."

"Twins?" Declan and I both say in unison.

"Mmmhmmm. I'm five months," she mutters around a roll as Blake ushers her to her seat.

"Here you rest, I'll grab some food."

"Thanks," she gives us a sheepish smile as she sits and devours her roll. *Seems like everyone can have babies but me.* Declan squeezes my shoulder as if he knows what's going through my mind. He kisses my temple before filing into the line to make his plate. I watch Pop, Declan's Dad, with Gage and can't help but smile. That man was meant to be a Pop for sure. He loves kids and they love him.

After dinner Isabella went home with Kate and Mason so Declan and I tackle the kitchen together. We work in a companionable silence for a while before I finally get the nerve to say something.

"Declan, I'm scared."

"Of what babe?"

"I've lied to you," I look away as a tear runs down my face.

"About?"

"I'm sick. I need to make an appointment, but I'm afraid. I don't want to be sick. I don't want to die."

"Heather," he wraps me into his arms and holds me there for a moment as we stand in our kitchen. "Baby, it could be nothing. It could be something, but I know you are strong and you're capable of defeating anything that comes your way."

"I wasn't able to defeat not being able to carry a baby."

"That isn't something we could help, baby."

"Neither is cancer."

"Heather, I don't think you have cancer. I think you're just afraid of what it could be and I think you need to go to the doctor."

"I will I promise." I reach up and kiss his lips while sliding my hand into his five o'clock shadow. I whimper as the prickly skin leaves my hand tingling.

"You trying to distract me woman?"

"Is it working?" I bite my lip as I stand back and pull my dress over my body and dump it onto the floor, revealing a peach colored bra and matching lace thong. The growl that erupts from his lips sends a shiver down my body before he slides his own shirt off.

"Hell yes it's working." His lips press against my own as he slides his tongue over mine asking for entrance. When I give it to him his hands grab my ass and lifts me until my legs are wrapped around him. I can feel just how much it's working and I can't help but be satisfied that this amazingly sexy man wants me.

He walks down the hallway and throws me onto our bed. I watch as he strips himself and then rips the lace of my panties and pulls away what's left. Arching my back, I unhook the bra and throw it on the floor just in time for him to press his bare chest against mine. We swallow each other's moans as he joins us once more, making us both forget all the things we were discussing. Making us remember just how much we belong together. Nothing else matters when it's just the two of us like this, and it's one of the greatest feelings I will ever have.

Chapter 8

Declan

Watching the family gather around the Christmas tree at Dad's is something that I cherish. Watching Isabella get to spend time with the family is a lot of fun. She and Matthew are only a couple of months apart and watching my brother's son grow up with my daughter is something I will cherish because my brother isn't here to watch it happen with.

Mason and Kate had made the announcement that they were expecting and were about three months along. I was extremely happy for them, but in a way I wasn't. What was it about Heather and I that prevented God from letting us be parents? Yes, I knew that Isabella was my chance to be a father and I loved her with everything inside of me. But, I would have liked us to have a child with our blood running through their veins. A child who looked like my wife and myself, a piece of Heather to always have with me, in case something ever happened to her.

"Daddy, can we open a present?" Isabella asks, her face shining so brightly that it's impossible to ignore.

"You'll have to ask your mother," I flick her nose with the tip of my index finger before she takes off running to her mom. I couldn't help but smile as her little voice rang out through the house. Even at five years old, the child was a ball of energy. I wish I had that much energy, or that I could bottle it up to save for later.

Looking at Heather, running around trying to get everyone's things was unnerving me since she was looking worse these days. She covered the black under her eyes with makeup so that no one else would notice that she wasn't sleeping. She'd been losing weight but her stomach was starting to poke out more, which she'd told me was because she was bloating and had finally admitted to me that she was afraid she had a tumor or something.

I broke down that night and prayed for my wife. I just sank to my knees, bowed my head and begged God to not let it be cancer. To heal her and help her, or to at least give her the courage to seek help. I loved her, but I wouldn't push her to do something she didn't want to do. And, if I was being honest I was just as afraid as she was at the thought of losing her.

"You, son, are a very lucky man," my father's voice booms out beside me. That man has never been able to whisper, if he was two hundred feet away from you, you'd still be able to hear him.

"Yes I am, Dad."

"I wish your mother was still here to see all of this, but in a way I'm glad she left the world before your brother."

"I don't think she'd have handled it well, Pop."

"She wouldn't have. God knows things, I suppose," he gives me a sad smile. "I sure do miss them both."

So do I, Pop. So do I," I grab his hand and squeeze it as I look over at my wife and think about just how lucky I am. I can relate to my dad when it comes to losing a child but I can't imagine what it would be like to lose the love of your life.

Heather smiles at me from behind the bar as she grabs the tray of drinks and starts to lift it. As if time stands still, I watch her make a pained face, before the tray flies over her and she collapses to the floor.

"Heather?" I scream as I run into the kitchen, pulling her into my arms and assessing her for harm. "Heather!"

"Here, let me through," Mason's voice booms as he pushes past Pop and Kate and stands beside me. He's on call today and I am thankful more than ever that the man decided to move here instead of staying back in Hickory with his friends. He checks her wrist for a pulse. "She's still breathing, so that's good." He shines a light into her eyes from some small flashlight that seemed to have magically appeared in his hand. "Pupils are dilated but she's not responding," he mutters as he reaches for his radio on his shoulder. "10-45C, sister-in-law, en-route to Main Street Hospital."

"What did you just say?" I ask him as he helps me stand.

"Look, her eyes aren't responding to anything, something isn't right. We need to get her to the hospital, Dec." He gives me a sad smile as he takes her and rushes to his car. I follow him as if my body is on autopilot, my mind not really able to comprehend the seriousness of the situation. He hands her to me before he opens the backdoor to his police car. "Climb in the back with her and keep trying to talk to her, see if she makes any type of response," he yells as he waits by the back door waiting for me to get in. After I climb in, the door slams shut and he jogs to the driver's side. He flicks the lights on and in a matter of seconds we are on the road to the hospital.

"Heather? Baby?" I ask with a shaky voice, trying to get her to wake up. "Come on baby, wake up for me." I don't even realize I'm crying until I see the drops of water on her face. I wipe them off her face and try to calm myself down. I didn't even think about Isabella seeing her momma pass out on Christmas Eve of all nights. I guess it's a good thing that we were surrounded by family.

"Keep talking to her, we're almost there," Mason calls from the front as he takes a wide turn.

"I don't know how in the heck you listen to those sirens so long," I run my fingers through Heather's hair, trying to do anything to get her to come back to me.

"You get used to it, but with everything going on lately in the world, I feel like I'm wearing a damn target on my back more often than not," he mutters as he takes another sharp turn, pulling into the hospital and slamming it into park right in front of the entrance. He climbs out of the vehicle and opens the door for me to get Heather out, she's still not awake and it's making me nervous as hell.

"Help! Emergency!" Mason screams out as we run into the emergency room, I've never been more thankful for him than I am right now. Had we just been a normal couple walking in, we might not have gotten back there as quickly. They take Heather from me, leaving me feeling emptier than I ever have.

"Mr. Jackson, I'm Nurse Hannah, Mason informed of the situation. I am going to need you to tell me what happened. Also, I need you to fill out this paperwork on your wife." The woman standing in front of me gives me an encouraging smile as I take in her appearance. She's got light brown hair pulled into a ponytail and wearing red scrubs with reindeer all over them.

"We were visiting with my Dad for Christmas Eve and Heather, she well, she was running around doing what she does at every event. I tried to tell her to take it easy before we got there, something has been off for a few months."

Amanda Lanclos

"A few months? What do you mean sir?"

"She's been having more problems sleeping and eating lately. She thinks she's hiding it from me," I run my hand over my face, looking at the kind woman. "I've not wanted to push her to see a doctor because, well she's stubborn and I didn't want to start a fight with her."

"I see," her kind smile turns into a condescending frown and I try my best to not get angry. *Who is she to judge me?*

"Well, she had a family member who battled cancer and lost, so if I was in her shoes I wouldn't want to find out the worst either. So don't give me that look," I mutter before Mason smacks me on the back, in warning.

"Sir, I apologize. I know what it is like to have a loved one fear something. Not just my own, I see it every day here. I didn't mean to pass judgment," she says quickly, rushing her words and handing me the clipboard with the papers on it. "If you'll fill these out for me as soon as I get word on your wife, I will come and let you know."

"Thank you," I say softly as I turn to find a not so comfortable spot in the nearly empty waiting room to fill out the paperwork.

Two hours I sit in that room, staring at the cream walls until they blur and repeat the process. Mason got called out to another job but Dad is here. He'd gone to get coffee. Kate wanted to be here, but we needed someone to stay with the kids. I start thinking the worst when my name is called. I sit up with a jolt as a man with greying temples and a kind smile walks over to me. My eyes take in his white coat, his green scrubs and his tennis shoes.

"I'm Declan Jackson," I say softly as I stand, waiting for the worst.

"Mr. Jackson, I believe we have some news," he gives me a small smile. "Heather is awake now. She took quite a spill and may have a concussion. She didn't want to hear anything without you present, so if you wouldn't mind following me."

"Yes sir, thank you." I smile knowing that for now, at least, she is awake and I get to see her smile at me, at least another day.

Chapter 9

Heather

Sitting in this uncomfortable bed, twisting my fingers in my lap while I wait is hard to do. I'd woken up in this bed in this atrocious gown and freaked out. I couldn't find Declan and I was afraid. The last thing I remember was everyone sitting around the tree laughing and then, here I am.

"Heather, I'm Lacey, I'll be your nurse. Can you tell me the date of your last menstrual cycle?" The perky upbeat redhead says as I think back.

"I have irregular cycles so I really can't remember the last one I had," I mutter trying to think hard about the last time I had one, but I keep coming up blank.

"That's okay. We ran some tests and the doctor will be in to see you shortly," she gives me a huge smile and starts to leave, but before she does I speak.

"Wait! I don't want to hear anything without my husband."

"Of course, I will have someone get him for you. In the meantime, would you like something to eat or drink?"

"Please, my throat is so dry."

"I'll bring you some juice and something for your head. I'm sure it's hurting."

"Yes, now that you mention it," I say touching the sore spot on my head and wincing. "Ouch!"

"You took a pretty big spill, we will make sure you're taken care of though," she smiles as she walks out of the room.

I look up when the door opens again, revealing my very sexy and disheveled husband. "Hi," I smile weakly as the other man steps in behind him. My stomach drops as the man meets my eyes with a small smile of his own. *My life is about to change forever; I'm fixing to be given a death sentence.* The monitor on the wall starts to beat erratically and I curse under my breath.

"Well hello Mrs. Jackson. I'm Doctor Phillips. I have some news I'd like to share with you and your husband if that's okay with you two." He sits down on the chair as Declan comes and sits on the bed by my pillow, running his fingers through my hair.

"Yes sir," I reply softly while reaching for Declan's hand.

"It's going to be okay, no matter what I will be here every step of the way." Declan's rough voice whispers into my ear, before he pulls away and kisses my temple. He may not realize what he's doing but he's giving me every ounce of strength I need to be able to get through the horror of this moment. The moment when I find out that I am going to die. My stomach flutters and I know then that it's a sign that I am going to hear bad news.

"Mrs. Jackson, I haven't done an ultrasound yet, but we have done blood work. You're pregnant." The doctor says the words and I look at him like he's insane.

"Pregnant? No, I can't be pregnant. We can't have a baby," I stutter and Declan is sitting there stunned.

"Well, your hCG levels in your blood are very high, signifying that you are around almost four months pregnant."

"I don't understand. I thought all the sickness and not sleeping and vomiting was from cancer. I've had six miscarriages. Doctors have told us that we likely wouldn't even be able to conceive." I feel the little kick in my stomach again and I gasp. "It kicked me."

"Well I can understand why you wouldn't think it was a pregnancy. If you'd like to see your baby, we can send you to ultrasound?"

"Okay." Declan and I both say at the same time. "I'd like to know how far along I am. I have never been able to carry past sixteen weeks."

"Sure thing, I'll go put the order in. Congratulations on the new addition. It's Christmas and miracles happen, you will deliver this baby and have a new member in your family," he says with firm determination as he walks out of the door.

"Declan, a baby?" I squeal. Not really sure what to do, we weren't planning on this, but it's an unexpected and very welcome surprise.

"A baby, I'm so excited."

"You don't seem so excited."

"I'm still in shock," he admits before running a hand over his face. "It's been so long since we tried, I am afraid to hope," he whispers as he looks into my eyes. I know exactly what he's saying.

"I know you are baby, but I think it's going to be different this time. Here give me your hand," I reach for him as he puts his hand near mine. I put his hand on my stomach and silently wish for the baby to move again like it did earlier. When I feel it, I see the awe in Declan's face and I can't help but smile bigger.

"It just kicked me!" He squeals with excitement as the door opens and the nurse comes in with a portable machine.

"We didn't want to chance you falling again tonight. You're going to have to have a better diet to get you back on track with your weight and make sure the little one stays healthy. But, anyway I'll wait until later to hassle you on that. Let's take a look and see how far along you are. I just need you to lift your gown for me. This may be a little cold." Lacey gives me a big smile as she squirts the jelly onto my skin, before putting the little wand up against my stomach and the screen fills with a baby. One that is bigger on that screen than any I have been able to see before.

"Oh wow," Declan mutters and the sobbing begins from me again.

"It looks like according to the growth on the chart here, he is measuring at nineteen weeks and two days," she says before turning to look at me. "Would you like to hear the heartbeat?"

"YES!" Both Declan and I shriek at the same time.

"Wait did you say he?" Declan's question makes me think and I look at Lacey.

"I did, if you'll look right here, you'll see his little well you know," she laughs softly as she points to the little thing that looks like a turtle. As she laughs, his strong heartbeat fills the room. I can't help but breakdown again as I realize that I am further along in this pregnancy than I ever have been. Even though I am terrified and worried that I could lose him at any minute I know that this is a gift. A very pleasant gift that may have been unexpected, but if I knew

Amanda Lanclos

anything, it's that any blessing in life comes when you least expected it.

Epilogue

Heather

"Declan!" I say his name, shaking him as I try to roll out of the bed. "Declan!" I screech a little bit harder. "Wake up!"

"What? What?" He jolts up in the bed and looks around. f I was sure this was pee I was sitting in I might even try to seduce him with how good he looks with his messed up hair and cute face. "Are you okay? Why's the bed wet?" He lets out an exasperated sigh. "Bladder fail?"

"No! I didn't wet the bed. I think it's time," I say softly. "My water broke," I try to get out of the bed but the pain that rocks through me steals my breath and I tense up.

"Baby?"

I hold my hand up, almost as if saying wait a second. "Contraction."

"Oh Shit! It's happening? He's coming!" He jumps up from the bed, runs to the closet, grabs some pants and a shirt and throws them in my direction before dressing himself. If I weren't in so much pain already I might laugh at the comical aspect.

"Declan, it's okay baby, we've got time. Stop panicking." I wince because the pain is becoming unbearable, but I don't want him to know I'm hurting.

"Heather! You're about to have a baby! It's going to come out of your vagina! How the heck are you saying it's okay! I'm scared for you!" His eyes are the size of saucers and he's breathing erratically. I can't help but burst out laughing. My belly is bouncing heavily and he's freaking out even more. "Stop laughing! You're going to laugh him loose! Dammit I shouldn't have watched those dang YouTube videos on childbirth!"

"Declan, it's okay. I'm going to change my clothes, use the restroom and we can go. Can you take the sheets and stuff off the bed and throw them in the washing machine? Call Kate and get her to come get Isabella or get your Dad to come over?" I give him a smile as I take the clothing and walk to the bathroom, biting the inside of my cheek as another contraction rips through me. *Two minutes apart.* I continue to count the seconds after the pain eases. I use the potty, change into the pants and shirt he threw at me and then walk out of the bathroom.

"Thanks, see you in a bit, Pop." I smile as I see him running around throwing stuff into a bag. *Two minutes.* He looks up and sees me bending over to ease the pain and stalks over to me, leans over and picks me up. "Come on beautiful, let's get you into the car so we can go as soon as Dad gets here."

"Declan," I huff out through clenched teeth. "I'm okay, I'm just in labor."

"You are one strong woman then," he mutters as he loads me into the front seat of the truck. "There's Dad now, let's go." He climbs behind the steering wheel and peels out of the driveway. *Well if Isabella was sleeping, she isn't anymore.*

"I can't wait for Isabella to see him, she's going to be such a good big sister," I smile as I think about the moment the two of them will meet. It's going to be a beautiful experience.

He drives like a crazy man even though there is no traffic at two in the morning. I just cling to the door handle and pray that we make it to the hospital in one piece. He throws the car into park at the emergency room entrance and we are whisked into the room.

"Declan! I will kill you for this," I scream out as I push harder. My whole body is shaking as it works hard to get our son out to greet the world. I really wouldn't ever kill Declan, but when my water broke the labor seemed to progress so fast that I had to forgo the epidural. Another unexpected event in this pregnancy, but I can't complain because I finally get the very thing I prayed for.

"Come on baby, you've got this! Push! He's almost here!" Declan hoots as he holds my hand and stares down between my legs. "You look so beautiful," he says softly as he kisses my head.

"We are almost there Heather, just a couple more pushes on the next contraction and I think little Trenton will be here," the doctor says as she looks between my legs again. "He's got a head full of brown hair too," she smiles as another contraction hits me, ripping through my body and causing me to howl in pain. Declan winces as I lift myself again, pushing once more and smiling a huge smile when our son's cries fill the room. I sob as they lift him into the air, showing me the most beautiful thing I have ever seen. Life - something that I created with my husband out of love, and now I had a beautiful baby boy to show me just what purpose I had here.

"He's beautiful," I sigh as they take him to get cleaned up.

"Just like you," Declan gives me that smile, showing off the dimple in his right cheek and making me fall in love with him all over again. On May 23, 2016 our lives changed forever. Trenton Matthew Jackson was welcomed into the world and it was a memory I will forever cherish. Life for the two of us was something that never really got old. We had a beautiful daughter who was as much ours as her

Amanda Lanclos

little brother was now. It was full of twists and turns, but nothing was ever expected, and I was okay with that. I was okay with my life and having it be as crazy as it was, and I looked to several more years of the unexpected.

Acknowledgements

First off, thank you! The reader who purchased this book and read it, even if you didn't love it. Thank you for believing in me and taking a chance on me.

Thank you to my friend Lacey Black, who always helps me when I need a path to write a book. We bounce ideas off each other and we always see the light at the end of the rainbow. Thank you for helping me on my own path to success.

To my editor, Joanne Thompson! Thank you for everything! You do so much for me and on my crazy schedule. I love you for it all.

To my formatter, Brenda Wright with Formatting Done Wright, thank you so much for always working with my crazy schedule and for letting me know when I've forgotten to add something. You truly are an amazing lady and I don't know what I would do without you!

To my betas Kim Merow Lewis, Corinne Brinkley, Kristin Marvin, Nikki Costello and Melissa Lemons, I thank you from the bottom of my heart. You tell me when something plain out sucks. It makes my words better and makes me better. Thank you all for all of your hard work, because I couldn't do it without you.

Amanda Lanclos

About the Author

Amanda is from a small town near Baton Rouge, Louisiana. You can find her rooting for her Tigers every Saturday night when its football season. She is the mother of two babies, a boy and a girl. She has always had a love of books and reading, but never expected to become someone who would have others read her words. Her book series is known as The Wounded Souls and follows a group of people who have problems in their lives that could potentially make or break them. She also has a Christian Inspirational Series called The Unwavering Faith Series. She is the owner of Crazy Cajun Book Addicts blog and also coordinates the Booking in Biloxi Signing in Biloxi, Mississippi.

If you don't catch her on social media, she loves to hear from readers via email at authoramandalanclos@gmail.com.